Eenie Meenie Manitoba

Playful Poems from Coast to Coast

Written by Robert Heidbreder

Illustrated by Scot Ritchie

Kids Can Press

To my mom and dad — with many thanks also to the students, staff and parents of General Gordon School, Vancouver. — R. H.

Text copyright © 1996 by Robert Heidbreder
Illustrations copyright © 1996 by Scot Ritchie

Kids Can Press acknowledges the financial support of the Ontario Arts Council, the Canada Council for the Arts and the Government of Canada, through the BPIDP, for our publishing activity. **Canadä**

Kids Can Press Ltd.
29 Birch Avenue
Toronto, Ontario, Canada
M4V 1E2

Edited by Trudee Romanek
Designed by Marie Bartholomew
Printed in Hong Kong by Wing King Tong
Company Limited

CDN   96 0 9 8 7 6 5 4 3 2
CDN PA   00 0 9 8 7 6 5 4 3 2 1

Canadian Cataloguing in Publication Data

Heidbreder, Robert

Eenie meenie Manitoba : playful poems from
coast to coast

Includes index.

ISBN 1-55074-301-5 (bound)   ISBN 1-55074-818-1 (pbk.)

1. Canada — Juvenile poetry.   2. Children's poetry, Canadian
(English).* 3. Rhyming games — Juvenile literature.
I. Ritchie, Scot.   II. Title.

PS8565.E42E45 2000   jC811'.54   C99-932272-9
PR9199.3.H443E45 2000

Kids Can Press is a Nelvana company

On Your Mark . . .

Get ready for some read-along, rhyme-along fun! *Eenie Meenie Manitoba* is full of lively poems and funny characters that will make you want to giggle and wiggle and join in their play. Shimmy and shake with Ogopogo, skip with some Nova Scotia lobsters, and rhyme your way across Canada.

You'll find poems you can bounce balls to — under and over, up and around. Others make great skipping rhymes. Some are perfect for doing actions, others for playing clapping games with a partner. And when it's time to pick teams or decide who is "It," just choose a choosing rhyme. Many of the rhymes in *Eenie Meenie Manitoba* have a symbol or two like the ones below to get you started.

ball-bouncing   skipping   actions   clapping   choosing

But the symbols don't mean there's only one way to play with these poems. Try making up your own games. Add some actions to a skipping rhyme. Make up a silly dance for another. Think of a funny way to chant your favourite poem with some friends. No matter how you like to play, the poems in *Eenie Meenie Manitoba* can add to your fun. So go ahead: turn the page, read a rhyme, and start playing.

Great Bear Lake Bears

Get up! Get up!
You sleeping mound.
Great Bear Lake bears are marching down!
They want to tickle you to bits,
To tickle you to tickle fits,
To tickle you to wormy wiggles,
Squirms and snickers,
Wriggles, giggles,
To tickle you out of your heap,
To tickle you from lazy sleep.

So rise and shine.
Jump into play.
Great Bear Lake bears are on their way!

Great Bear Lake is a large lake near the Arctic Circle.

4

Shoo-Fly Pie

Blackberry, blueberry
Make a pie.
Gooseberry, salmonberry
Shoooo! Horsefly!

Huckleberry, brambleberry
Bake the pie.
Boysenberry, raspberry
Shoooo! Deerfly!

Bearberry, buffaloberry
Cut the pie.
Twinberry, thimbleberry
Shoooo! Blackfly!

Strawberry, mulberry
Eat the pie.
Crowberry, cranberry
Shoooo! Housefly!

Skip to this poem on your own or with some friends. Each skipper can choose one flower name to jump out on. Then everyone can jump back in for the last line.

Daisy Faye

Daisy Faye from Garden Bay
Ate fresh flowers every day
From her dogwood breakfast tray:

Lady's slipper, pitcher plant, hollyhocks,
Sunflower, violet, forget-me-nots,
Dandelion, foxglove, fireweed,

Until one day Faye went to seed!

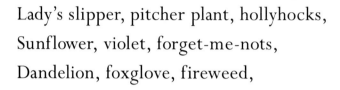

Inken Tinken

Inken Tinken wildlife
Lost your horse in Yellowknife.
Inken Tinken gander goose
Rode instead a hairy moose.
Inken Tinken moose got stuck,
Took a Tuktoyaktuk truck.

Try "skating" as you bounce your ball.

On the Rideau

2 – 4 – 6 – 8
On the Rideau go and skate.
If you fall, a snake's your date.
2 – 4 – 6 – 8

Taxi Max

Taxi Max from Halifax
Had a fleet of Cadillacs.
Filled them up with lobster snacks
Wrapped in farmer's almanacs.
Sent the snacks off with a fax
To pay up all his income tax!

The Candy Store

I met Laura Secord.
She gave me a cow.
The cow didn't moo.
She gave me a shoe.
The shoe was too big.
She gave me a wig.
The wig was too long.
She gave me a song.
The song didn't sing.
She gave me a ring.
The ring wasn't handy.
She gave me a candy.
The candy was great.
I asked for eight.
She said, "No more!
I'll open a store."

Zed to Bed

A B C D E F G
Grabbed a train in wild B.C.
H I J K L M N
Nodded off to Newfoundland.
O P Q R S and T
Toppled into the salty sea.
U V W X Y Zed
Zipped right home and went to bed!

According to folklore, Laura Secord and her cow walked 30 km to warn the Canadian commander of a surprise American attack during the War of 1812.

Words of Warning

Ogopogo shimmy
Ogopogo shake
Don't dive deep in the Okanagan Lake.

Sasquatch roar
And Sasquatch rail
Don't stray off that mountain trail.

Ogopogo scrunch
And Sasquatch crunch
You'll be an Ogopogo-Sasquatch brunch!

Ogopogo and Sasquatch are two mythical Canadian monsters.

Eenie Meenie Manitoba

Eenie meenie Manitoba
Go and catch a Brandon cobra.
If it bites you in the tum,
Then you have to wave your thumb.
If it bites you on the toes,
Then you have to pull your nose.
If it bites you on the head,
Then you have to go to bed.
If it bites you in the eye,
Then you have to kick and cry.
But if it bites you on the knee,
Run to Winnipeg with me.

WINNIPEG

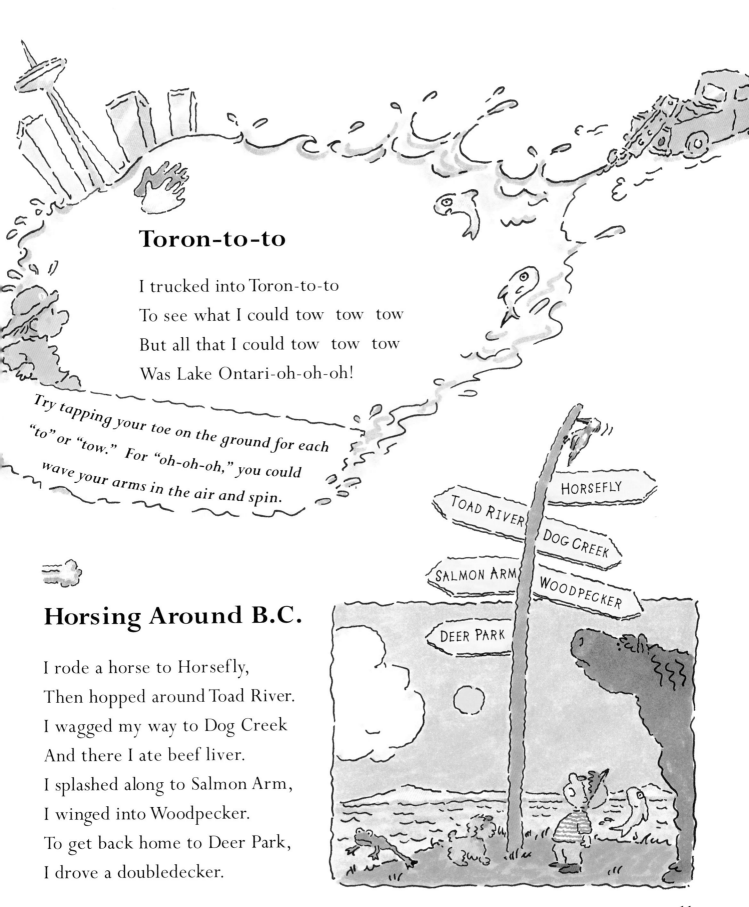

Toron-to-to

I trucked into Toron-to-to
To see what I could tow tow tow
But all that I could tow tow tow
Was Lake Ontari-oh-oh-oh!

Try tapping your toe on the ground for each "to" or "tow." For "oh-oh-oh," you could wave your arms in the air and spin.

Horsing Around B.C.

I rode a horse to Horsefly,
Then hopped around Toad River.
I wagged my way to Dog Creek
And there I ate beef liver.
I splashed along to Salmon Arm,
I winged into Woodpecker.
To get back home to Deer Park,
I drove a doubledecker.

Charlottetown Fishmongers

Charlottetown fishmongers
Chop fishes' heads,
Slide them under
Townspeople's beds.
Town cats find them,
Have them for supper,
Spice them up with red-hot pepper!

On the word "pepper," begin skipping as fast as you can. How long can you keep going?

Valentine Dance

1 2 3 4
Please be mine
5 6 7
My valentine
8 9 10
And dance with me
From P. E. I. out to B.C.

10 9 8
We'll heel and toe
7 6 5
Waltz to and fro
4 3 2 1
Fling and spring
And home to P.E.I. we'll swing.

Lanky Hank

Lanky Hank
From dank Cold Bank
Ate hot onions till he stank.
Dove in the sea and down he sank,
Popped back up near a freighter tank.

How many onions stank up Hank?

This poem ends with a challenge. How many times can you jump before you trip? You can count onions as you skip.

Bird Time

One o'clock
Two o'clock
Loon fly by.
Three o'clock
Four o'clock
Gull loop high.
Five o'clock
Six o'clock
Heron swoop down.
Seven o'clock
Eight o'clock
Tern poke around.
Nine o'clock
Ten o'clock
Murre come play.
Eleven o'clock
Twelve o'clock
Puffin swim away.

Flap your arms and "fly" about as you mimic the birds in this poem.

14

Monday's Child

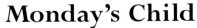

Monday's child's a humpback whale.
Tuesday's child's a lobster tail.
Wednesday's child's a marshy moose.
Thursday's child's a snowy goose.
Friday's child's a wet coho.
Saturday's child's a buffalo.
Sunday's child's a caribou . . .
      who'd rather be a kangaroo!

This Tree

This black oak leans to the right.
This white birch soars out of sight.
This yellow willow creaks and sways.
This grey elm's seen stronger days.
But this red maple's wide and high.
We'll climb its green and reach blue sky.

How fast can you say this poem?

Sledsledfast

Sledsledfast
Bobsled
Janesled
Off the mattress on the bed

Sledsledfast
Bobsled
Janesled
Past their baby brother Ted

Sledsledfast
Bobsled
Janesled
Slicing up banana bread

Sledsledfast
Bobsled
Janesled
Under skitty kitty Fred

Sledsledfast
Bobsled
Janesled
Round the rooms from A to Zed

Winter Weather Watch

What weather's in the West today?
Snow, snow — come what may!

And on the Prairies? Out that way?
Snow, snow — buckets they say!

And by the Great Lakes? Round there, eh?
Snow, snow — without delay!

And in Quebec what's under way?
Snow, snow — a white soufflé!

And in the Maritimes today?
Snow, snow — in every bay!

But what about up north, I say?
Snow, snow — it's there to stay!

Dig out your skis, snowshoes, your sleigh,
Your slick dogsled,
Go out and play!

Dog-Gone Rose

Dog rose
Hound rose
Round and round the world goes.

Grow a rose with coffee.
Grow a rose with tea.
Grow a rose with your toes
And nose it home to me.

Rose dog
Rose hound
Rosily the world goes round.

This is called a circular poem because it keeps going around and around and around . . .

Bear-Go-Round

A grizzly tagged a polar bear.
The polar tagged a brown.
The brown tagged a black bear,
Turning into town.

The black tagged the grizzly bear.
The grizzly tagged the brown.
The brown tagged the polar bear,
Roaring round and round.

The polar tagged the black bear.
The black bear tagged the brown.
The brown tagged the grizzly,
Tearing out of town.

Then,
The grizzly tagged the polar bear.
The polar tagged the brown . . .

Apple Me Dapple Me

Apple me dapple me on my feet
Down a dapple sauce apple sauce street.

Apple me dapple me on my knees
Over the dapple juice apple juice seas.

Then apple me dapple me on my head
Home to a dapple pie apple pie bed.

Between ball bounces, try touching your feet, then your knees, and finally your head as you say this rhyme. Can you touch with both hands?

Sugar Maple

Sugar maple, sugar maple,
Drip your sap,
From your springtime
Maple tap.

Then boil up, boil up,
Bubbly sap,
For maple syrup
CLAP, CLAP, CLAP!

For maple sugar
SNAP, SNAP, SNAP!

Wiggling fingers make good dripping sap. Try rolling your hands around each other for the boiling and bubbling parts of this poem.

Peppermint Moose

A ginger sheep	*(clap your hands twice)*
And a nutmeg mare	*(tap your shoulders twice)*
Danced all night	*(roll your hands around each other)*
With a cinnamon bear.	*(roll your hands again)*
The cinnamon bear	*(clap your hands twice)*
And a cardamom goose	*(tap your shoulders twice)*
Played all day	*(thump your thighs for a running moose sound)*
With a peppermint moose.	*(thump your thighs again)*

Do the actions as you read this poem. How fast can you go?

Nova Scotia Lobster

Nova Scotia lobster touch the ground.
Nova Scotia lobster turn around.
Nova Scotia lobster do high kicks.
Nova Scotia lobster do the splits.
Nova Scotia lobster stamp the floor.
Nova Scotia lobster slam the door,
Then dance back in and start once more.

As you "slam the door," jump out so the next skipper can jump in.

Simmy's Salmon

Simmy caught a salmon.
"Look at my chum!"
"No, it's a pink,"
Shouted her mum.
"No, it's a coho,"
Cried out Dad.
"Sure it's a sockeye,"
Shrieked Uncle Brad.
"Bet it's chinook,"
Screamed Auntie Plum.
But Simmy didn't care.
Her salmon was her chum.

*You can read this poem with some friends
and take turns being different characters.*

You're the King

You're the king.
You're the queen.
You're the grand old duke.

The king wears mitts.
The queen a scarf.
The duke a dirty tuque!

Tugboat

Tugboat,
Kayak,
Leaky canoe,

Down
Sink

Y,
O,
U!

Croony June

Croony June
From Saskatoon
Clapped wheat beats in the afternoon,
Tapped wheat feet in the harvest moon,
Boomed wheat tunes on a brass bassoon —

One tune, two tunes, three tunes, four,
Until she moved to Labrador.

Ready, Set, Raven

Raven on the mountain,
Raven in the tree,
Raven up the windy sky,
Can't catch me.

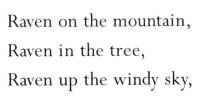

You can
use this poem to start a race
Everyone runs on the word "me."

Wheat to Eat

Manitoba wheat
Saskatchewan wheat
Plant it with your fingers,
Stamp it with your feet.

Alberta sun
Manitoba rain
Grow the wheat to golden grain.

Saskatchewan mills
Alberta power
Grind the wheat to silky flour.

Prairie bakers
Oven heat
Bake good bread for me to eat.

Kinnikinnick-a-Knock-Knock

Kinnikinnick-a-knock-knock,
What's over there?
A berry hungry baby bear.

Kinnikinnick-a-knock-knock,
Where's its mum?
Berrily off filling her tum.

Kinnikinnick-a-knock-knock,
Where's its dad?
High in the hills — he's berry mad.

Kinnikinnick-a-knock-knock,
Why's it leaving?
It's berry full of berry thieving!

Kinnikinnick
*(pronounced kin**nick**-kin**nick**),*
or bearberry, is a common
berry shrub of the
Pacific Northwest.

Try telling your future with this poem. Pull the petals from a daisy as you say the words. Or form a circle with your friends and say the poem as one person points to each of you in turn.

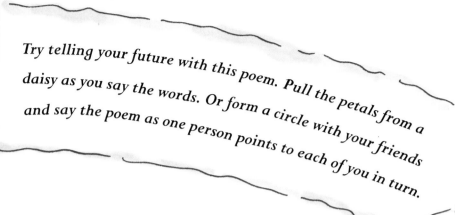

To Be or Not to Be

Poet Potter Illustrator
Teacher Preacher Decorator
Carpenter Gardener Car mechanic
Pacific Prairies or Atlantic

Fisher Dancer Math professor
Banker Farmer Tax assessor
Miner Logger Hockey star
Bush plane Bicycle Antique car

Doctor Lawyer Computer whiz
Stock market Government Big showbiz
Plumber Skier Figure skater
Marry never, now or later.

28

Crow Days

One crow on Monday,
    laugh and play.
Two crows on Tuesday,
    peace all day.
Three crows on Wednesday,
    friends abound.
Four crows on Thursday,
    a lost wish found.
Five crows on Friday,
    fall in love.
Six crows on Saturday,
    clear skies above.
Seven crows on Sunday,
    never a care.
But no crows at all —
    Beware! BEWARE!

Lull-a-Blue-Bye-Bye

Bluenose schooner,
Please buy me a tune
To lull me to sleep
Under blue-eyed moon.

Spin me soft songs
On silvery seas.
Roll me round waves
On a rock-a-bye breeze.

Wake me fresh dreams
Through saltwater night.
And smooth-sail me
Into sun-eyed light.

Northern Lights Wish

Northern lights,
Bright ribbon sights,
Wrap up for me my wish tonight.

Tie a bow,
Not too tight,
For me to open at day's light.

Sleep All Night

Snowshoe hares
Have gone to bed.
Wrap up tight.
Lay down your head.

Narwhals rest
In icy deep.
Close your eyes.
Go to sleep.

Caribou
Are snowy warm.
All is safe,
Away from harm.

Northern skies
Are full-moon bright.
Dream soft dreams.
Sleep all night.

Index of Poem Titles